THE SMURFS 2

Gargamel the Great

adapted by Tina Gallo
illustrated by Dynamo Limited

Ready-to-Read

Simon Spotlight
New York London Toronto Sydney New Delhi

SIMON SPOTLIGHT
An imprint of Simon & Schuster Children's Publishing Division
1230 Avenue of the Americas, New York, New York 10020
SMURFS™ & © Peyo 2013 Licensed through Lafig Belgium/IMPS.
The Smurfs 2, the Movie © 2013 Sony Pictures Animation, Inc. and Columbia Pictures Industries, Inc. All Rights Reserved.
All rights reserved, including the right of reproduction in whole or in part in any form.
SIMON SPOTLIGHT, READY-TO-READ, and colophon are registered trademarks of Simon & Schuster, Inc.
For information about special discounts for bulk purchases, please contact Simon & Schuster Special Sales
at 1-866-506-1949 or business@simonandschuster.com.
Manufactured in the United States of America 0513 LAK
First Edition
1 2 3 4 5 6 7 8 9 10
ISBN 978-1-4424-9025-3 (pbk)
ISBN 978-1-4424-9026-0 (hc)

It is a beautiful night in Paris, France.
Gargamel the wizard is getting ready
to perform his magic show.
He admires his reflection backstage.

Gargamel struts onstage
and greets the cheering crowd.
"Good evening, unworthy admirers!
I am Gargamel the Great.
Prepare to be amazed!"

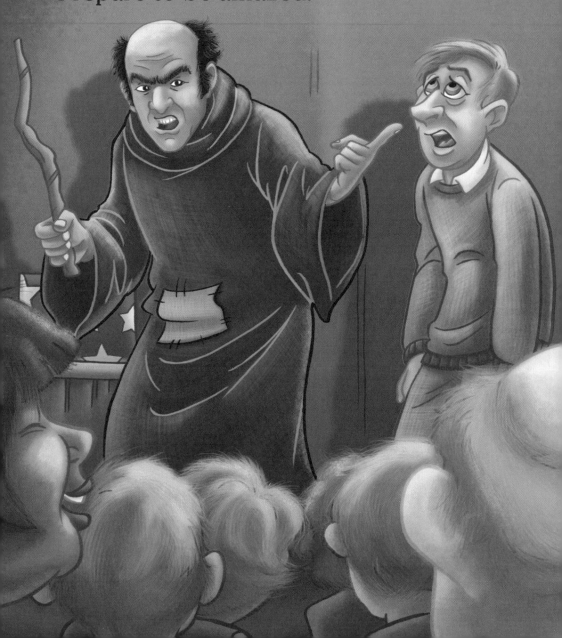

Gargamel asks for a volunteer.

A man walks onto the stage.

Gargamel begins to work his magic.

"Say you belong to Gargamel," he says.

"You belong to Gargamel," says the man.

The audience laughs.

Gargamel is furious.

"You are a dimwitted toad," he says.
"You are a dimwitted toad," the man
repeats.
"No, YOU are!" Gargamel shouts.
Gargamel waves his wand
and bright blue light comes out of it.
The man turns into a giant toad!
The audience gasps!

Gargamel's cat, Azrael, meows offstage.
The toad hears the cat
and shoots out his long, sticky tongue.
He slurps Azrael up!
Gargamel yells at the toad's stomach.
"Azrael, are you dead?"

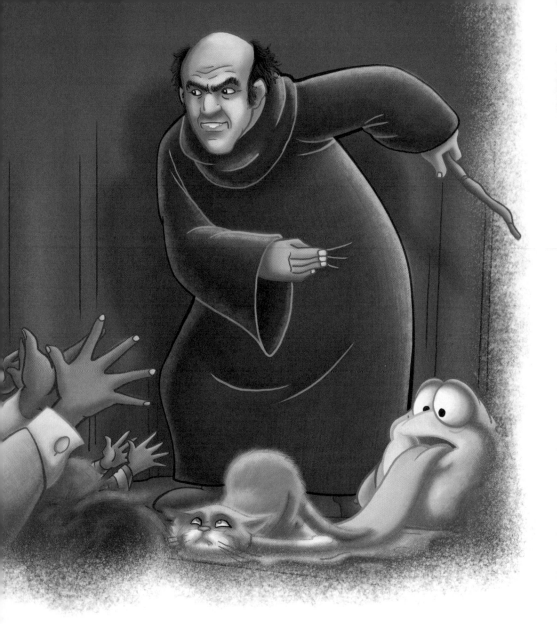

Inside the toad's belly, Azrael meows.
"Get out of there!" Gargamel yells.
The toad spits out the cat.
The audience cheers.
Gargamel takes a bow.

Every night after his show,
fans wait at the stage door
to see Gargamel.

Gargamel looks at the crowd.

"Get on your knees and bow," he says.

The crowd laughs.

"I said BOW!" Gargamel shouts.

Gargamel waves his wand at his fans.
He puts them under a spell.
They all fall to their knees and bow.
"That's better," Gargamel says.
As soon as he leaves, the spell is over.
His fans all stand up and cheer.
They like being a part of the show.

To perform his magic Gargamel needs
blue essence from the Smurfs.
He wants to collect enough essence
to use his powers to take over the world.
He decides to make his own Smurfs so he
can extract their essence.

He kidnaps Smurfette so she will tell him
the secret formula to make Smurfs.
Smurfette will not give him the formula.
But Gargamel still needs
blue essence to perform his magic!
So he cuts off some of Smurfette's
hair to produce enough for his next show.

Gargamel steps onto the stage.
There is a light mist around him.
"I wanted the fog of mystery!" he screams,
and waves his wand.
A huge gray fog cloud fills the stage.
Everyone applauds.

Azrael is now much bigger than a tiger!
The crowd cheers.
Gargamel smiles.
"And now I need a volunteer.
Who would like to put his head
in the kitty's mouth?"
The crowd is silent.

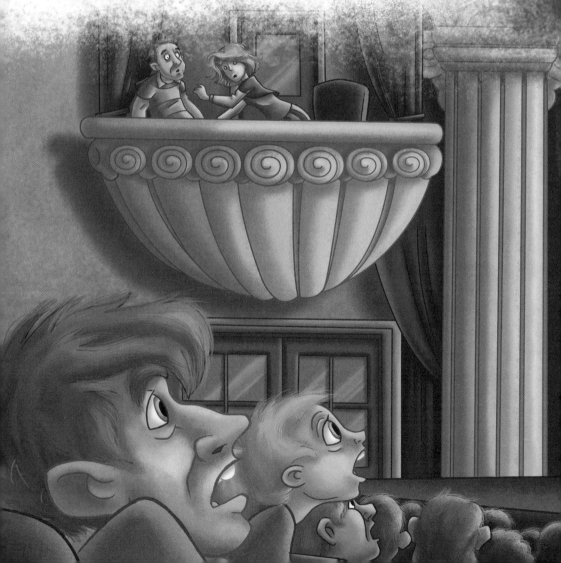

Azrael walks across the stage.
People stop applauding and laugh.
Gargamel gets angry at the audience.
"Stop that! Why do you giggle?"

A man in the audience explains.
"Your cat is very small.
Usually a magic show has big cats,
like lions and tigers. . . ."

Gargamel nods his head.
"If it is a big cat you want,
your wish is my command."
Gargamel waves his wand.

Gargamel tries again.

"Don't worry, he just ate!

At the very worst you'll lose an ear!

Any volunteers?"

Suddenly there is a noise
in the audience.
It is Patrick and Victor!
They are friends of the Smurfs.

They live in New York.
They have come to Paris
to try to save Smurfette
from Gargamel.

Victor yells, "Where is the Smurfette?"
Gargamel gets angry.
He raises his wand.
"Duck!" Patrick yells.

Confused, Gargamel yells back, "Duck?"
Gargamel's magic changes Victor
into a duck!

Then Gargamel smiles at Patrick.
"It appears we do have a volunteer,"
he says.
Gargamel waves his wand
and Patrick flies to the stage,
right toward giant Azrael!

Gargamel turns to the cat.
"Open wide, Azrael," he says.

The giant cat roars and opens his mouth.
He is about to swallow Patrick!

But Victor the duck flies in front of Gargamel to protect Patrick.

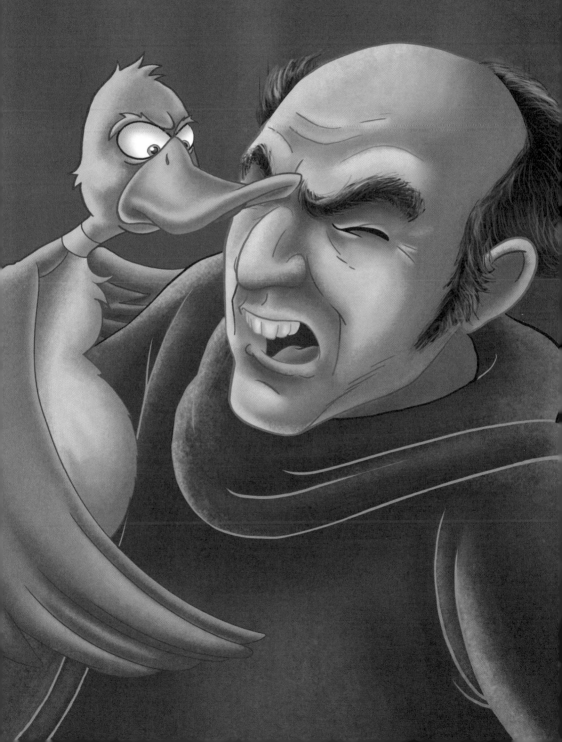

Victor knocks Gargamel down
and Gargamel accidentally
waves his wand in front of Azrael.
Azrael turns back into a normal cat.

The audience cheers.
They think it is a wonderful trick!

Patrick and Victor the duck
run out of the opera house.
Gargamel realizes he must
find Smurfette and hide her from them.

The audience cheers.
They think it is a wonderful trick!

Patrick and Victor the duck
run out of the opera house.
Gargamel realizes he must
find Smurfette and hide her from them.

If they save Smurfette, Gargamel will
run out of blue essence, and will not
have power for his magic show.
"The show is over,"
Gargamel tells the audience.

Gargamel takes a grand bow.
"Good-bye! Come back tomorrow to see
another performance by
Gargamel the Great—I hope!"

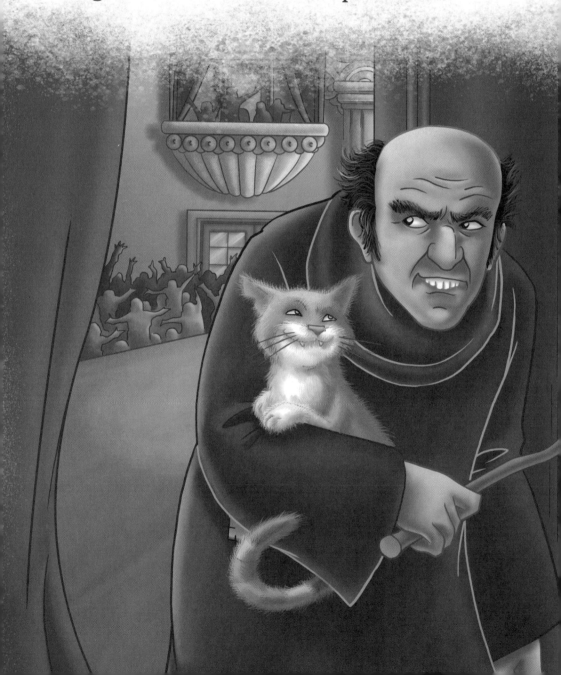